D0601651

Good Night, Garden Gnome

JAMICHAEL HENTERLY

Dial Books for Young Readers ❧ New York

Good night,
Garden Gnome.

For Ann Marie,
because she imagined.

And for Diane Arico,
because she believed.

Published by Dial Books for Young Readers
A division of Penguin Putnam Inc.
345 Hudson Street
New York, New York 10014

Designed by Lily Malcom
Printed in Hong Kong on acid-free paper

1 3 5 7 9 10 8 6 4 2

Library of Congress Cataloging-in-Publication Data
Henterly, Jamichael.
Good night, garden gnome/by Jamichael Henterly.
p. cm.
Summary: A gnome comes to life at night to work in his garden.
ISBN 0-8037-2531-0
[1. Gnomes—Fiction. 2. Gardens—Fiction. 3. Stories without words.] I. Title.
PZ7.H39875 Go 2001
[E]—dc21   99-087548

The images in this book were painted with
watercolors on Arches hot-pressed paper.